*For Nanna Betty
and her handbag full of
dog biscuits.*

PEACHTREE PUBLISHERS
1700 Chattahoochee Avenue
Atlanta, Georgia 30318-2112
www.peachtree-online.com

Text and illustrations © 2012 by Alex T. Smith

First published in the United Kingdom in 2012 by Hodder Children's Books
First United States version published in 2013 by Peachtree Publishers

Artwork created digitally. Title is hand lettered; text is typeset in Italian Garamond BT.

Printed and bound in 2013 in China by RR Donnelley & Sons
10 9 8 7 6 5 4 3 2 1
First Edition

Library of Congress Cataloging-in-Publication Data

Smith, Alex T., author, illustrator
  Claude at the circus / text and illustrations, Alex T. Smith.
     pages cm
  Summary: While Mr. and Mrs. Shinyshoes are away for the day, Claude, a small, plump dog, and his friend, Sir Bobblysock, share adventures in the park and at the circus.
  ISBN: 978-1-56145-702-1 / 1-56145-702-7
  [1. Dogs—Fiction. 2. Parks—Fiction. 3. Circus—Fiction. 4. Humorous stories.] I. Title.
  PZ7.S6422Ckm 2013
  [E]—dc23
                                        2013000896

CLAUDE

at the Circus

ALEX T. SMITH

PEACHTREE
ATLANTA

Chapter 1

In a house on Waggy Avenue,
number 112, there lives a dog.

A small dog.
A small, plump dog.
A small, plump dog who wears a
beret and a rather fetching sweater.

His name is Claude, and here he is.

beret

rather fetching
sweater

Claude's best friend is Sir Bobblysock. He is both a sock and quite bobbly.

Sir Bobblysock

Claude and Sir Bobblysock don't live in their big house all by themselves; Mr. and Mrs. Shinyshoes live there too.

Usually, Mr. and Mrs. Shinyshoes
get up bright and early, leap into
their smartest clothes and shiniest
shoes, and hotfoot it out the door
to work. Sometimes though, mainly
on nice sunny Saturdays, Mr. and
Mrs. Shinyshoes pop on their comfy
clothes and pack a picnic.

7

"Let's go on a day trip!"
Mr. Shinyshoes says.
"Lovely idea!" says Mrs.
Shinyshoes. "Shall we take
Claude?"

"No," whispers Mr. Shinyshoes.
"Let's leave him here to sleep.
You know how awfully tired he gets.
We won't be long."

And so Mr. and Mrs. Shinyshoes
tiptoe out of the house,
hop in the car, and ramble off
to the countryside for the day.

But Claude hasn't really been
asleep. He's been listening with
his floppy ears and peeping
with his beady eyes.

As soon as the front door closes,
Claude jumps out of bed, puts on
his beret, and decides what
adventure he will have.

9

Chapter 2

One bright Saturday morning when Mr. and Mrs. Shinyshoes were off in the country, Claude popped on his beret and thought about what he wanted to do. He felt like he needed a treat as he had been very busy the day before, giving his bed a good spring clean.

He had plumped up the pillow,
shaken the blanket, and tidied
up his top-secret hidey-hole.

Out went several packages of half-
chewed cookies and a juicy bone
baguette, which was rather past
its best.

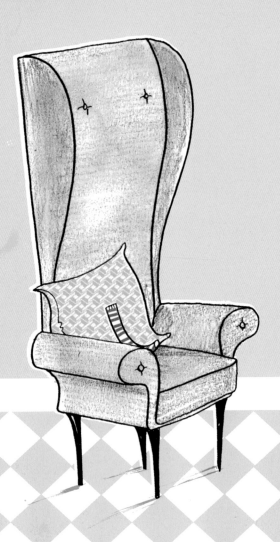

12

Sir Bobblysock had sat in a comfy armchair and told him what to do. He would have loved to help, but he didn't want to get in the way.

"I think I will go to the park today,"
Claude said.

So off he went.

Sir Bobblysock came along too,
although he was worried that all the
flowers might set off his hayfever
and make him sneeze.

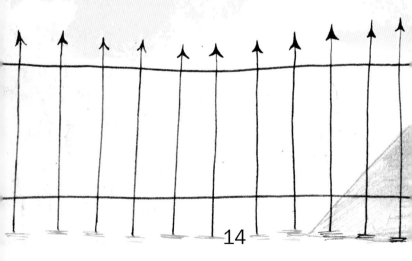

Chapter 3

Claude had never been to the park before.

He was surprised by how much like a big yard it was. There was grass absolutely everywhere, and several trees too.

And as it was such a sunny day, the whole place was full of people enjoying themselves.

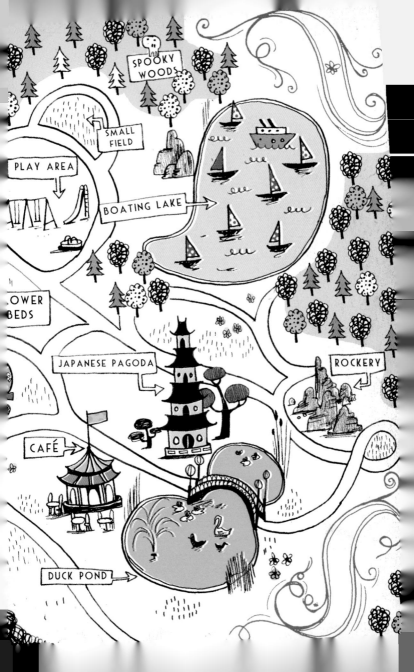

Claude was pleased to see there was also a van selling ice cream.
His tummy rumbled. Even though it wasn't quite eleven o'clock, he decided it was time for a snack.

But just as he and Sir Bobblysock stepped onto the path, a group of people in very strange clothes ran past them.

Claude had never seen anything like it.

There were even some people running with their babies in buggies!

Before he could say "excuse me" or ask politely what they were doing, he found himself tangled up among them.

Soon, he and Sir Bobblysock were
jogging along with the group.
Sir Bobblysock had to hop like
crazy to keep up.

Around and around the park they
went, running all the time.
Claude quite enjoyed it, but he
did wonder what on earth they
were running for.

Had a lion escaped from the zoo?

Were all these people being chased
by the police?

Maybe everyone had realized they weren't wearing proper clothes and were running home to get changed.

Claude didn't know.

What he did know was that his tummy was still grumbling and now he couldn't even see the ice cream van. There was no other option but to escape from all these crazy running people.

Quickly, he tucked Sir Bobblysock under his arm, and was just about to leap out from the crowd when his foot got caught in one of the joggers' dangly shoelaces.

Everyone went flying. Claude and
Sir Bobblysock hurtled through the
air, bumped down on the grass, and
tumbled over and over until...

...they landed neatly in a flower bed!

It was very comfortable there and the flowers smelled lovely.

Claude looked around and decided the flower bed would be the perfect spot to take a nap. After all that running around, he and Sir Bobblysock were very tired.

Forgetting all about ice cream, Claude settled down and closed his eyes. Sir Bobblysock, who always found sleeping in sunlight difficult, popped on his eye mask and took some deep breaths to relax.

Chapter 4

But the nap didn't last very long.

"Ahem! Ahem!" coughed a man in a sharp uniform and a peaked cap. It was the park keeper, and he did not look happy.

Claude and Sir Bobblysock woke up.

Sir Bobblysock was not pleased.
He always liked to nap
for exactly forty-six
minutes, and he had
only managed five.

The park keeper didn't say anything. He just pointed to a sign that Claude hadn't seen earlier, when he had been flying through the air.

SLIGHTLY IMPOLITE NOTICE

DO **NOT** SLEEP IN THE FLOWER BEDS

THANK YOU

33

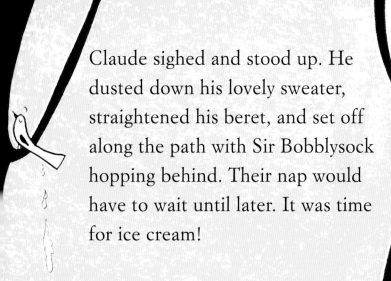

Claude sighed and stood up. He dusted down his lovely sweater, straightened his beret, and set off along the path with Sir Bobblysock hopping behind. Their nap would have to wait until later. It was time for ice cream!

Claude spotted the ice cream van in the distance.

"Come on!" he said to Sir Bobblysock, and marched toward it.

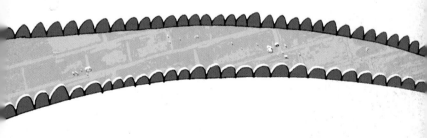

On the way, they found themselves striding across a funny sort of field. There were holes everywhere in the grass and somebody had littered the place with balls.

Claude quickly filled up the holes and tidied the balls away under his beret.

Some very rude people didn't seem very happy about what he had done, so Claude and Sir Bobblysock quickly scampered away to the ice cream van.

17TH

37

When they got there, Claude bought himself a vanilla ice cream with raspberry sauce. Sir Bobblysock really wanted a cup of tea but had a sticky, stripy popsicle instead.

After they had finished, Claude put
Sir Bobblysock's popsicle wrapper
in the garbage.

He also threw away another piece
of trash he had found stuck to a
bench, wanting to be helpful, and
not wanting to get told off by the
park keeper again.

They were wondering what to do
next, when someone whizzed by on
a scooter. And then someone else
whizzed by.

It looked like fun, so Claude and
Sir Bobblysock watched as the two
children zipped here and there,
doing tricky tricks and daredevil
stunts.

"Would you like a ride?" asked the little girl.

Claude nodded politely and climbed onto the scooter. He was a bit wobbly at first but was soon zooming around like nobody's business!

Sir Bobblysock had a turn, but he didn't enjoy it. He much preferred having a nice sit-down and a cookie.

Claude was just about to hand the
scooter back to the little girl
when he heard a noise from behind
him. It was somebody shouting...

Chapter 5

A baby suddenly zoomed past!
One of the running mummies
had let go of her buggy!

The baby looked very happy,
but he was heading straight for the
duck pond.

"Quick!" shouted the little girl.
"Save him!"

Claude grabbed Sir Bobblysock and
set off.

Sir Bobblysock took control of the handlebars, Claude pushed off with his foot along the path, and within a minute they had caught up with the escaped baby.

Claude reached out and caught the baby just before he fell in the water.

The baby was a bit miffed because he had been enjoying his ride.

Everyone clapped and shouted,
"Hooray for Claude and Sir
Bobblysock!"

Claude pulled the balls he had
tidied up earlier out from under his
beret and gave them a quick juggle.
Then Sir Bobblysock did a high-
stepping jig.

Everyone laughed and cheered again, but Claude was beginning to feel rather shy so he and Sir Bobblysock went to find the café for a spot of lunch.

They were sitting outside, munching happily, when a very strange-looking man came and sat at the table next to them.

Claude did his very best not to stare, but of course Sir Bobblysock couldn't help himself. He turned right around in his seat and had a good look. The man at the next table noticed.

"Hello," he said, holding out his hand. "I am the Amazing Alan, of Alan's Amazing Circus. May I offer you and your friend two tickets for this afternoon's performance? Ringside seats, on the house!"

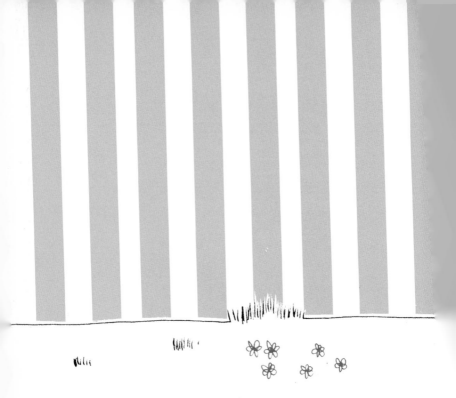

Chapter 6

Claude was delighted, as he'd
never been to the circus before.
He and Sir Bobblysock decided to
go to the circus tent early, to explore.

They ducked under the striped
canvas.

All the performers were getting
ready for the show in their trailers,
so there was no one around.

57

Claude couldn't help noticing that although the tent was very exciting, it was also very untidy and quite grubby in places.

There was only one solution. He would have to give the tent a jolly good spring clean.

Claude fished a feather duster out
from under his beret and dusted the
ring. Then he swept all the sawdust
on the floor into a big pile in the
center. He climbed a long ladder
and gave the trapeze a good polish,
and the high wire a once-over with
a damp cloth.

Behind a curtain, he found a pile of plates covered in fluffy custardy cream. Claude decided the cream smelled a bit funny, so he threw it away and washed the plates.
Soon they were all neatly stacked in a pile, sparkling clean.

By now the rest of the audience had started to come in, so Claude and Sir Bobblysock took their seats. The Amazing Alan waved to them, but he had to hurry off to help the Human Cannonball find her glittery crash helmet.

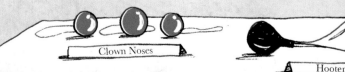

Clown Noses

Hooter

61

Claude and Sir Bobblysock watched in amazement as acrobats and gymnasts and dancers and clowns came tumbling into the ring. They were all dressed in wonderful costumes. Sir Bobblysock, who liked sequins and feathers and that sort of thing, was very impressed. The Amazing Alan cracked his whip, and the show began.

Chapter 7

But it was a disaster!

The clowns weren't funny at all. Their custard pies had been washed away, and when they threw the clean plates at each other they ended up with sore noses.

The trapeze artists were no better. The trapezes were so slippery that they couldn't keep ahold of them, so they landed with a bump in the sawdust and bruised their bottoms.

The audience began to realize
something was wrong.

The tightrope walker slipped off the damp wire and dangled by her underpants until their elastic snapped. Then she fell onto a trampoline, bounced through the tent roof, and landed in the duck pond.

People in the audience began to
mutter. The Amazing Alan was very
embarrassed.

"This has never happened before,"
he said to Claude and Sir Bobblysock.
"I've got no idea what's wrong with
my performers today."

Claude did, and was beginning to feel
a bit hot behind the ears.

"Would you take over?"
Alan asked. "Otherwise, I'm
afraid the audience will ask
for their money back."

Claude was astonished.
He had never performed
in a circus before.

"Don't worry, you'll be brilliant,"
said Alan. "I saw you juggling in
the park. Here, wear this hat.
And take the little fellow with you –
he's funny."

So Claude and Sir Bobblysock
found themselves standing in the
middle of the ring...

Chapter 8

At first Claude wasn't sure what to do, so he just smiled politely and wagged his tail.

"Get on with it!" hissed the Amazing Alan, who was watching nervously.

Claude smiled again, then he did some jumping jacks and some twirls.

The audience was impressed.

Then Claude cleverly rubbed some chalk on the bottom of his shoes, so his feet wouldn't slip.

He clambered up the ladder and stepped onto the tightrope.
It was ever so high, so he shut his eyes and pretended he was just tip-toeing down a very thin bit of road.

To his surprise, he found that he was quite good at it. He hung from one paw and stood on one leg (not at the same time).

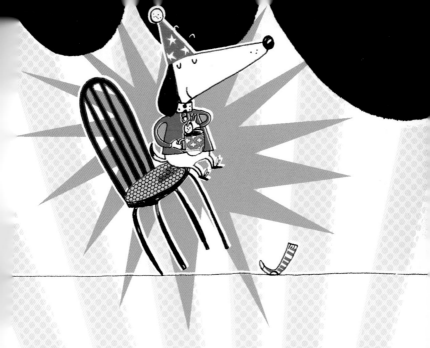

Then, because he was getting tired,
he sat down halfway along and
drank a cup of tea. The crowd went
wild when he dunked his cookie.

Next, Claude and Sir Bobblysock did a clown routine. They whizzed around the ring in a car that was too small for them, and fell over a lot.

Then they threw some freshly made custard pies at each other. The pies were so delicious, Claude couldn't help catching one in his mouth and gobbling it up, plate and all.

The audience thought this was very funny.

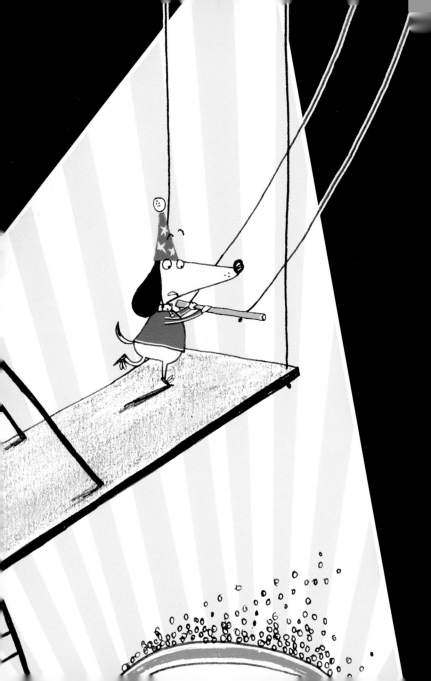

Finally, it was time for the trapeze act.

Bravely, Claude and Sir Bobblysock climbed up the ladders, reached for a trapeze each, took a deep breath, and swung out over the audience.

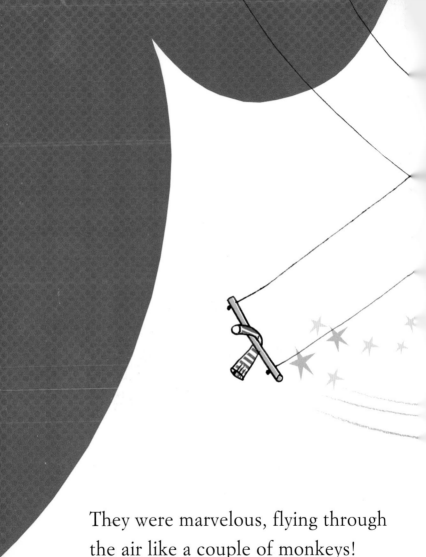

They were marvelous, flying through
the air like a couple of monkeys!

Everyone leaped to their feet and
clapped until their hands were sore.
"Hooray!" they cried. "Hooray for
Claude and Sir Bobblysock!"

Chapter 9

The Amazing Alan was delighted. "You are both absolute stars!" he boomed, as Claude and Sir Bobblysock took a bow.

"Please will you join our circus? You will be very famous if you do!"

Claude thought for a moment. Although circus life sounded fun, he would miss Mr. and Mrs. Shinyshoes too much if he went away. So he said thank you very much and that he had enjoyed himself a lot, but he would rather just go home. Besides, Sir Bobblysock was in need of one of his long naps.

Suddenly, Claude gasped. There was a problem! He had forgotten the time.

How could he get home before Mr. and Mrs. Shinyshoes came back from the country?

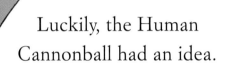

Luckily, the Human Cannonball had an idea.

As soon as Claude had said his goodbyes to all the friendly circus people, he put on the Human Cannonball's glittery crash helmet, tucked Sir Bobblysock safely into his sweater, and clambered into the huge cannon.

Claude flew through the air and landed with a *crash* in his cozy bed in the kitchen, just as Mr. and Mrs. Shinyshoes were opening the front door.

He quickly pretended to be asleep.

"Um... Mrs. Shinyshoes?" said Mr. Shinyshoes, looking at Claude. "Do you happen to know why Claude is wearing a glittery crash helmet?"

"No idea, darling!" said Mrs. Shinyshoes, looking up. "Do you know why there's a Claude-shaped hole in the roof?"

Mr. Shinyshoes said he didn't have a clue.

But Claude did, so he gave Sir Bobblysock a secret wink.

How to be a Clown

1. Paint your nose red with face paint.

2. Tell some silly jokes.

What kind of dog takes a bubble bath?
A shampoodle!

What swings from a trapeze and meows?
An acrocat!

Why do dogs wag their tails?
Because no one else will do it for them!

3. Fall over a lot.

TA-DA! You are now a clown!

Keep your eyes open for Claude and Sir Bobblysock.
You never know where they'll turn up next.

CLAUDE
in the City

A visit to the city is delightful but ordinary, until Claude accidentally foils a robbery and heals a whole waiting room full of patients!

$12.95 / 978-1-56145-697-0 / Spring 2013

CLAUDE
at the Beach

A seaside holiday turns out to be more than Claude bargained for when he saves a swimmer, encounters pirates, and discovers treasure! *$12.95 / 978-1-56145-703-8 / Spring 2014*